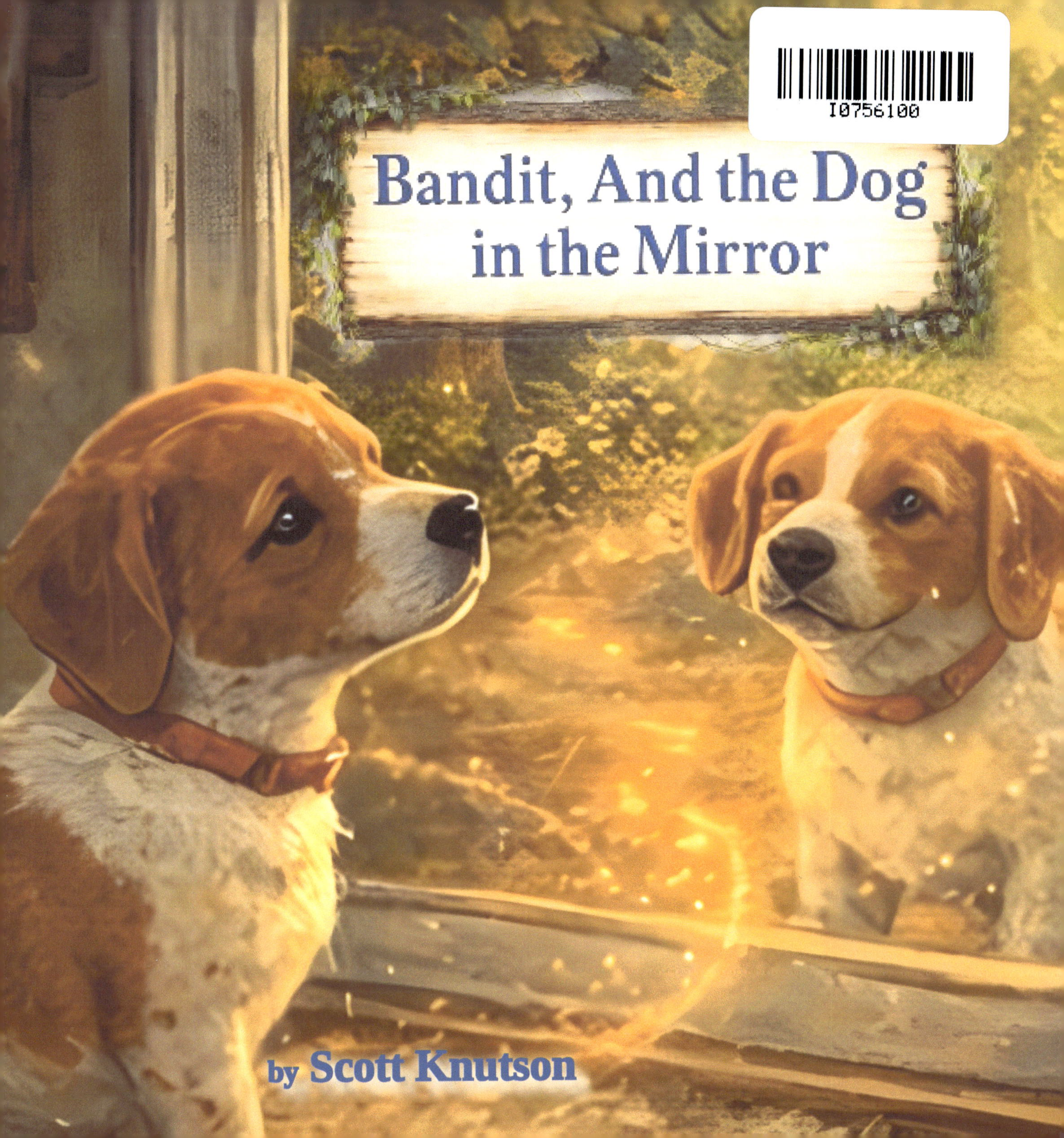
I0756100
Bandit, And the Dog in the Mirror
by Scott Knutson

To request permission, contact Scott Knutson scottknutson400@gmail.com

Cover Design: Scott Knutson and Prairie Hearth Publishing, LLC
Illustrated by Scott Knutson and Prairie Hearth Publishing, LLC

Graphic Design, Loretta Sorensen, Prairie Hearth Publishing, LLC
Edited by Loretta Sorensen, Prairie Hearth Publishing, LLC

ISBN: 978-1-969893-15-5
Printed in the United States

Published by Prairie Hearth Publishing, LLC, Yankton, South Dakota 57078

DEDICATION PAGE

For Bandit,
who showed us
that even the
smallest beginnings
can lead to the biggest adventures.

And for Rizzo,
the best big brother
a pup could ever have.

This book belongs to ______________________________

Signed, Bandit

In a quiet old barn
on a windy little farm,
lived eight tiny puppies,
all snuggled up warm.

But one little pup,
the shyest of all,
was Bandit, so tiny,
so quiet and small.

The world felt so big,
some nights felt so long,
and sometimes deep shadows
danced across the big barn.

Yet Bandit had something
deep in his heart—
a spark full of love,
right from the start.

One day kind, warm hands
came and opened the door.
New voices! New smells!
And something much more!

Bandit was scooped up,
gently and tight—
for the very first time
things felt perfectly right.

Out of all of the puppies,
who were playful and loud,
this shy little runt
stood out from the crowd.

“This is the one,” they said,
smiling so wide,
and Bandit knew love
had finally arrived.

Now Bandit had a home,
all cozy and sweet,
with soft comfy beds
and all he could eat.

And a big brother, too—
named Rizzo, Bandit found
who welcomed him warmly,
and showed him around.

Now, Rizzo, he was older,
strong, gentle, and wise,
with kindness shining warmly
in big brown caring eyes.

He showed Bandit the ropes,
how to run, jump, and play.
Bandit knew then for certain
he would be safe every day.

But Bandit had a habit,
a curious sort of way.
At the end of each night,
or the start of each day.

He'd sit so very still,
without making a sound—
staring quietly at something
when no one was around.

At the foot of his bed,
on the floor at nose-height,
was a closet door shining
very smooth and so bright.

And there in that mirror,
looking right back at him,
was a pup just like Bandit,
pretty small, white and tan.

Bandit tilted his head,
to the left, then the right.
The other pup copied him!
What an unusual sight!

“Who are you?” Bandit wondered,
trembling slightly inside.
“Are you my new friend?
Will you run by my side?”

As Bandit sat staring,
his nose gave a twitch.
That pup in the mirror
made the exact same switch!

“Do you smell that?”
Bandit thought with delight.
“Adventure is calling—
let’s follow it tonight!”

And suddenly—whoosh!
In his curious mind,
Bandit saw forests and trails,
new adventures of all kinds.

Tall trees to explore,
leaves crunching below.
And a long winding trail
where wild scents just might go!

Explorer Bandit,
brave even though small,
followed the trails,
clearly loving them all.

Over logs and through grasses,
so thick and so tall—
now he wasn’t the runt.
No, no! Not at all!

He sniffed out some secrets,
that were hidden away,
like where squirrels and chipmunks
run, hide, and play.

With each tiny clue
and each brand new smell,
Bandit's thoughts raced ahead
to the stories he'd tell.

Then, deep in the woods,
as he continued to roam,
he remembered the barn
he once had called home.

He’d been so small,
shy and easy to miss.
But there was more to his story,
so much more than this!

And there in the mirror,
side by side he would stay,
with his explorer pup friend,
full of joy, full of play.

Now strong and fearless,
courageous and true,
“Is that really me?”
Bandit wondered too.

Then blink! The big forest
faded from view,
and back in the room
was the mirror he knew.

But something had changed,
deep down inside.
Bandit the explorer
felt his heart fill with pride.

Back on the bed,
Rizzo watched from nearby,
with a gentle tail wag
and an all-knowing eye.

As if he could see
every trail bandit ran,
and believed in him deeply,
more than anyone can.

Because the pup in the mirror,
as Bandit could see,
was now brave and kind,
and full of such glee.

And the more Bandit looked,
the more he'd discover:
sometimes your best friend
is yourself in the mirror.

The Story of Bandit & Rizzo

Bandit and Rizzo are both rescue dogs
from a local organization we've grown to love
—Noah's Hope Animal Rescue.

Rizzo came first. He was one of three siblings…
right in the middle of the bunch!
My wife, Pam, named him after my favorite
Chicago Cubs first baseman, Anthony Rizzo.

A few years later, I had my heart set on getting a beagle. As luck would have it, Noah's Hope let us know about a litter that had come in from a nearby farm. They weren't fancy, papered dogs —but that didn't matter to me one bit.

The moment I saw Bandit —the runt of the litter —I knew he was the one. I've always been the kind of guy who roots for the underdog.

From the very beginning,
Bandit and Rizzo bonded in the best way.
They've always gotten along so well
and truly love each other
—playing, exploring, and sharing life side by side.

Scott Knutson lives in South Dakota where life is filled with music, family, and a couple of very special rescue dogs. With over 30 years in law enforcement and current work supporting Homeland Security's Federal Protective Service, Scott has dedicated his life to protecting and serving others.

When he's not working, Scott shares his love of music as a solo acoustic performer through his business, BrewCoustic Entertainment—bringing people together one song at a time.

Bandit and Rizzo were welcomed into our lives through Noah's Hope Animal Rescue, and their playful, curious spirits inspired this story. *Bandit, And the Dog in the Mirror* is a celebration of discovery, courage, and the joy of being exactly who you are.

www.ingramcontent.com/pod-product-compliance
Lightning Source LLC
LaVergne TN
LVHW070152110826
845147LV00002B/376

* 9 7 8 1 9 6 9 8 9 3 1 5 5 *